CHUGG

KOKO
THE SQUIRRELS

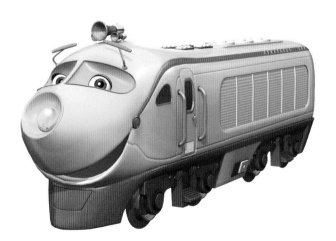

Bath New York Singapore Hong Kong Cologne Delhi Melbourne

One morning, Vee asked Koko to go to the timber yard.

"I can't wait! I'm ready for my tunnel colour Vee," Koko said excitedly.

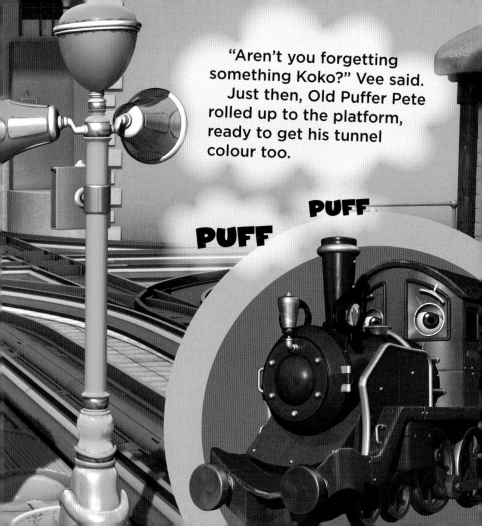

"Aren't you forgetting something Koko?" Vee said. Just then, Old Puffer Pete rolled up to the platform, ready to get his tunnel colour too.

PUFF

PUFF

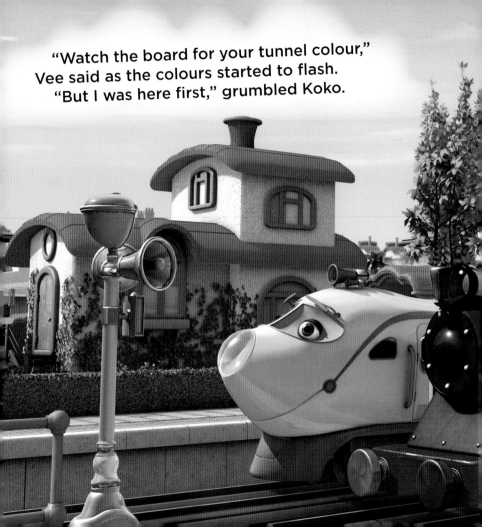

"Watch the board for your tunnel colour," Vee said as the colours started to flash. "But I was here first," grumbled Koko.

"When I was your age, this was all done with coloured flags," Pete said. Koko rolled her eyes. She had heard that story before.

"Is it my turn now?" Koko asked with relief when Pete had gone towards the green tunnel.

But Koko had forgotten a flatcar to carry the timber!
"Back in two clickety-clacks," she called.

CLICKETY
CLACK!

At the rolling stock yard, Dunbar tried to help Koko buckle up to a flatcar.

"Back up slooooowly," he said, but Koko was too excited about her day to stay still. It was boring to go slow.

"I'm going to chug-a-chug all the way to the timber yard and then chug-a-chug to the paper mill," she said.

Meanwhile, Old Puffer Pete was enjoying his trip, when two squirrels jumped onto his roof.

"Oh! Hello Mr. Squirrel," he said.

PUFF

PUFF

The large squirrel brushed his tail on Pete making the old chugger laugh. "Oooh, ho, ho, your tail is tickly," he chuckled before chugging away.

Back at the depot, Koko found out that her tunnel colour was green. It was the same as Old Puffer Pete's!

"I hope I don't get stuck behind Pete," Koko said as she sped away. It was too big an adventure to go slow!

Koko raced out of the tunnel.
"Woo-hoooo!" she shouted, zipping round the bend.
"Go Koko, go Koko, go Koko," she sang.

♪ "GO, KOKO, GO, KOKO!" ♪

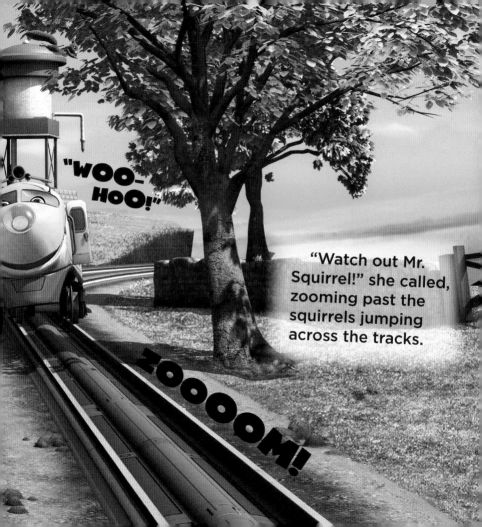

When Koko collected her load of timber, she raced to the paper mill. Suddenly, she saw a baby squirrel on the tracks!

SCREEEECH

As Koko slammed on her brakes, her load of logs tumbled to the ground.

"Emergency stop!" she shouted, and the squirrels hurried away from the rails. "I'm sorry I was going too fast. I didn't mean to scare you."

Old Puffer Pete had been right;
she should have been going slow and
steady. How was she going to pick the
logs up?

Then Pete came round the corner, on his way back from the foundry!

"Old Puffer Pete to the rescue!" he said, smiling at Koko.

PUFF PUFF

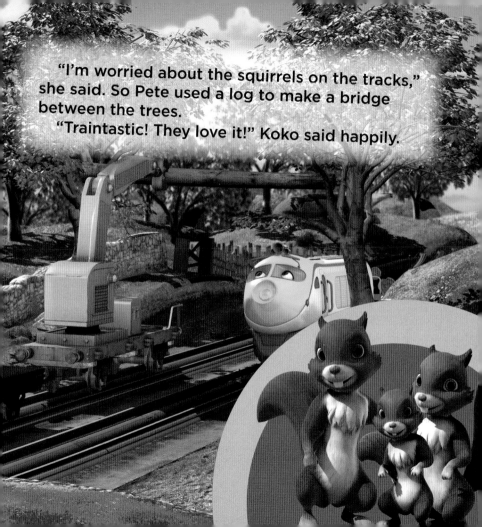

"I'm worried about the squirrels on the tracks," she said. So Pete used a log to make a bridge between the trees.

"Traintastic! They love it!" Koko said happily.

"Now I've learnt to always take it slow and steady," Koko said as they returned to the depot.

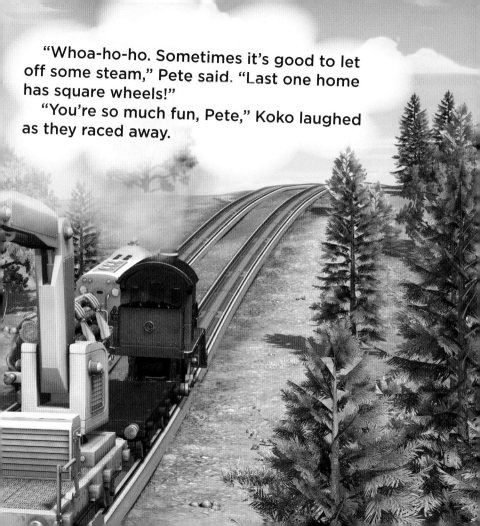

"Whoa-ho-ho. Sometimes it's good to let off some steam," Pete said. "Last one home has square wheels!"

"You're so much fun, Pete," Koko laughed as they raced away.

Can you spot the five differences between these pictures from the story?

Tick a box when you spot each difference!

1 2 3 4 5

What letter completes Koko's phrases from the story?

....hugga ....hoo

....hugga, ...hoo!

You ....an't ....atch Koko!

....lickety-....lack!

Answers: Chugga chugga, choo choo! You can't catch Koko! Clickety-clack!

Can you join the dots to complete this picture of Old Puffer Pete? Colour him in!

Which colour track will lead Koko to the timber yard?

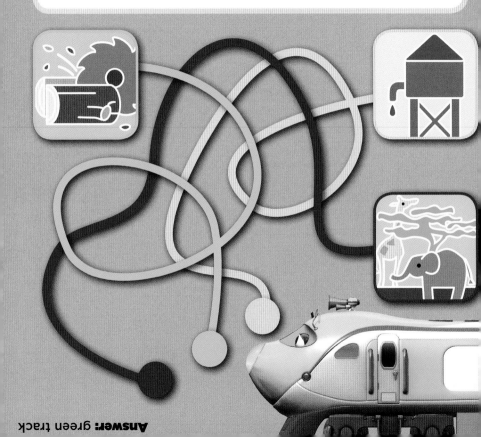

Make your own Old Puffer Pete!

1. Ask an adult to help you cut out the template carefully with safety scissors.

2. Fold the tabs inwards along the dotted lines.

3. Secure tabs with glue or sticky tape.

4. Add your stickers to each side.

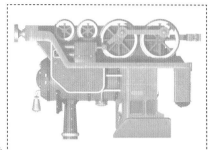

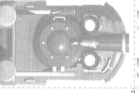
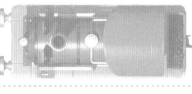
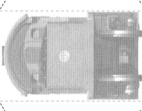

Complete your Chuggington collection.
Tick them off as you collect!

More chuggtastic books to collect!